Taurus the Octopus

and the Wise Old Tortoise

Written by Colin Macmillan

Illustrations by Tim Davis

AuthorHouse™ UK
1663 Liberty Drive
Bloomington, IN 47403 USA
www.authorhouse.co.uk
Phone: 0800.197.4150

Published by AuthorHouse 6/16/2015

ISBN: 978-1-5049-4363-5 (sc)
ISBN: 978-1-5049-4364-2 (e)

Print information available on the last page.

This book is printed on acid-free paper.

authorHOUSE®

Taurus, the brave octopus, was sick with boredom,

He ruled his home-world, the blue, salty ocean,

He was flexible and strong and used black ink as his weapon,

No creature could beat him, no creature was stronger,

But he couldn't stay here bored, for one second longer.

'I know, I'll go, where no octopus has gone
I'll go on an adventure, I'll go onto land!'

So he pulled himself from the watery sea
And marched on his eight legs, confidently
Planning to be back, in time for his tea.

I take it that's you off then?

But the octopus travelled far too many miles

He was puny on land, it was menacing and wild

And the noises that bellowed from strange land creatures

Who found the octopus ugly and queer

Made the strong swimmer tremble with fear.

The scorching sun, dried and burned him

And birds of all colours pecked at his skin

And big-bellied beavers gnawed on his limbs

And crazy baboons, beat and bit Taurus

But they themselves... got bored with the octopus.

The powerful octopus was hurt and frightened
As he'd never dreamt for all of this to happen
His adventure had become a living nightmare
He needed cheering up, he needed laughter
But he was far too weak to get back to the water.

The wind felt sorry, so she cooled his burns
And blew his sad whimpers across the lands
Where an old, wrinkled tortoise heard his cries
Which made the tortoise very angry deep inside
'Hold on Taurus, I'm coming,' he cried.

The tortoise moved so slowly, that he'd take too long
To reach the poor octopus, just in time
But the wrinkled old tortoise had his own weapon
Something he was best at, something he'd been given
Something he'd learnt, something called 'wisdom'.

You see, the old tortoise had listened to the songs
Of all the different animals that lived on the land
And after many, many years, after so, so long
The clever little tortoise could mimic and understand
All the types of languages, that jabbered and jiggled
and jumped around.

Parlez vous français?

Oui mon amie. Ça va?

The tortoise first 'neighed' his song to a greedy horse
Who'd gobbled too many truffles, that had grown from the earth
The horse picked the tortoise up into her mouth
And carried him gently, because he had once helped her
By feeding her foals, whilst she fought a fierce fever.

Maurice, pinch me!
I think I just saw a horse
carrying a tortoise...

The horse carried the tortoise for miles and miles
But because of her diet, she soon got tired
So she placed the tortoise onto the ground,
Then after wishing him the very best of luck
The fat old horsey, fell asleep in the muck.

The tortoise then 'chattered' his song to a monkey
Who thought the tortoise was hunky dory.

As he'd once bandaged the monkey's sore head
And baked the monkey some banana bread
'I'll help you tortoise' the monkey said.

So the monkey thought, 'what can I do?'
Then all of a sudden, he suddenly knew
He called to his chums, a gang of monkey builders
Who quickly, and nimbly, turned a tree into a boat
And off down the river, the tortoise did float.

But the strong river currents made the boat sprout a leak,

The quick monkey builders had made the boat too weak.

So the poor, old tortoise sank down to the river's bottom

Where a crocodile, with a rumbling tummy

Thought the tortoise looked really yummy.

The croc took a bite at the drowning tortoise

But as his teeth bit into the hard, tough shell

The crocodile let out one mighty 'YELL'

Instead of lunch he only got grief

As into the sky, flew the crocodile's teeth!

As the croc sobbed with sadness, the tortoise took pity
So the old, clever tortoise plucked a fig from a fig tree
And gathered herbs and spices and clean, spring water
And mixed it all together to stop the croc's toothache
With a marvellous, sweet, frothy, medicine-milkshake.

The tortoise poured the drink down the croc's large throat
Which rumbled in his belly and squeezed out a huge 'BURP'
With a pop and a zing and a whizz and a fizz
The medicine milkshake soon worked a real treat
As out of his mouth, sprung a new set of teeth.

The croc blushed bright red, he was so embarrassed
He'd tried to eat the tortoise and in return he got kindness.

So he called out over the river and flowers and marshes
To his tiny, little friends, a family of bird dentists
Who'd clean the croc's teeth, for bugs and insects.

With all of their might the birds clung onto the tortoise
And after flapping and fluttering, whilst singing in chorus
They finally reached the poor, poor octopus
Then the tired little birds all collapsed in a heap
And one by one, they fell fast asleep.

The tortoise was upset, he was really horrified

Peering down at the octopus , he deeply sighed

With his last strength, Taurus looked up and cried

'Take me home where I'm safe and strong

I've been venturing on land, for far too long!'

So the tortoise, flung the octopus, onto his shell

And plodded to the ocean so that Taurus could be well

And after slowly passing, rock, brook, creek and tree

The two new friends, made it eventually

To the sight and sound of the crashing, blue sea.

I see you came back then?

'You will once again, gather all your lost strength

But remember to never let this happen again

And all I say is, remember what you've been through

And never do what those naughty creatures did to you'

Bye Taurus, be a **good** boy now!

The tortoise boomed...

as he plodded little by little... out of view.

Taurus peacefully flopped into his warm salt bath
He was back where he belonged, he was safe, he could relax
And he'd now found a friend, that no other could match
The wise old tortoise, that had travelled to save him
Through love and kindness and patience and wisdom.

The octopus now took interest in things he used to ignore
Everything that slid, swam or hid on sand floor
So he went to octopus school, he went to every lecture
He listened and learnt and got cleverer and cleverer
Eventually becoming an octopus professor.

He learnt about everything, his brothers and sisters
To even learn about the lowest of creatures
The crabs, the water horses, the fishes and leeches
And Taurus learnt that no matter how small or strange
Although each was different, they were all much the same.

Lightning Source UK Ltd.
Milton Keynes UK
UKOW07f0613290715

256014UK00006B/18/P